Don't Be an Asshole
A comprehensive guide to handling today's touchiest subjects.

By: Jake Blatt

Table of Contents

Marriage - 76

Media - 77

Money - 78

Monuments - 79

Movies - 80

Music - 81

News - 82

People - 83

Police Brutality - 84

Politics - 85

Porn - 86

Prayer - 87

Presidents - 88

Protesting - 89

Racism - 90

Reading - 91

Religion - 92

Renewable Energy - 93

Rescue Animals - 94

Revolution - 95

Rights - 96

School Shootings - 97

Science - 98

School - 99

Introduction

This is the only piece of advice you'll ever need.

Don't be an asshole.

No matter the situation, the subject matter, or the people you're with.

Don't be an asshole.

That bears repeating. What you may be thinking is that, "yeah, I'm not an asshole, my opinions are correct! It's the other guy that's being an asshole!" The other guy is thinking the exact same thing. In that situation, with that person, on that subject matter.

Don't be an asshole.

There are two sides to every story. Say it with me now,

Don't be an asshole.

Abortion

If you think abortion is murder.
If you think abortion should be as easy as taking Advil.
If you think there is absolutely no nuance to the entire debate.

Don't be an asshole.

Abstinence

If you think sex before marriage is a mortal sin.
If you think choosing not to have sex before marriage makes
you a prude.

Don't be an asshole

Accountability.

If you don't think this is one of the biggest things missing
from the world.
If you don't think holding people accountable for their actions
would make the world a better place.

Don't be an asshole.

Aliens

If you think aliens run the world.
If you think aliens can't exist and we're the only beings in the entire universe.

Don't be an asshole.

America

If you don't think this is the greatest country the world has ever known.
If you think it's a guarantee that we stay that way.

Don't be an asshole.

Animal Captivity

If you think that there is no benefit or knowledge to be gained from animals in captivity.
If you think animals in captivity don't deserve to at least be content.

Don't be an asshole.

Appropriation

If you think you have the right to anything and everything of everyone else's culture.
If you think there's no way to use, respect, or honor someone else's traditions.

Don't be an asshole.

Automation

If you think automation is taking over the world and robots will one day destroy us.
If you think there aren't legitimate concerns about how automation will affect the workforce in years to come.

Don't be an asshole.

Black Lives Matter

If you think Black people don't have any right to be upset.
If you think this is the last protest that will ever need to
happen.
If you think this solves everything.
If you think it doesn't *at least* get us closer to solving
everything.

Don't be an asshole.

Books

If you think people that read are caught in the past.
If you think that everyone cares about all the books you read.

Don't be an asshole.

Cable TV

If you think you still need cable.
If you don't miss some of the things about having cable.

Don't be an asshole.

Cancel Culture

If you think any bad thought, tweet, comment, or anything
from your past should automatically cancel someone.
If you think there aren't legitimate reasons to be cancelled.

Don't be an asshole.

Cars

If you think your loud, lifted, coal-rolling truck is cool. If you think an electric car is perfect and has no negative impact on the environment.

Don't be an asshole.

Cartels

If you think cartels rule every aspect of the world.
If you think they do it better than a government.

Don't be an asshole.

Censorship

If you think censorship is anything other than a reduction in
freedom of speech and expression.
If you don't think that it can still be tempting and maybe even
positive in some situations.

Don't be an asshole.

China

If you think China is ever going to do anything that isn't in their best interest.
If you think there isn't a world where we can all co-exist.
If you think China is handling all of the issues perfectly.
If you think they shouldn't be held accountable for their decisions on world stage.

Don't be an asshole.

Chores

If you think it's a woman's place to do all the chores.

Don't be an asshole.

Climate Change

If you think that the climate isn't changing.
If you think that the USA can change and that completely solves the problem.
If you think the problem no longer has a solution.

Don't be an asshole.

Clothes

If you think loud clothes distract from the person.
If you think clothes aren't one of the first things to be judged.
If you think you actually give a crap what anybody else is wearing.

Don't be an asshole.

Comedy

If you think there's no room in comedy for opinions on social issues.
If you think comedy *must* have a place in social issues.
If you think comics need to "stick to comedy".
If you think there isn't a different scale when judging a comedian's comments.
If you think context is irrelevant when talking about jokes that seem in poor taste.

Don't be an asshole.

Communication

If you think global, high speed communication isn't one of the greatest tools of knowledge in the history of the world.
If you think it doesn't scare those currently in power.
If you think it can't be wildly inaccurate or easily manipulated.
If you don't think it needs to continue to grow.

Don't be an asshole.

Computers

If you don't think computers are one of the greatest inventions
ever.
If you think they are without flaw or limitations.
If you think that they can't simultaneously be our greatest
risk, and our greatest hope.

Don't be an asshole.

Conspiracy Theories

If you think the moon landing, JFK assassination, or 9/11 didn't happen.
If you think there isn't some truth to some of them.

Don't be an asshole.

Crime

If you think that the punishment shouldn't fit the crime.
If you think that the punishment *always* does fit the crime.
If you don't think there are too many laws.

Don't be an asshole.

Death

If you think there's absolutely nothing after death.
If you think there's absolutely a heaven and hell.
If you think anybody on this earth knows for sure.

Don't be an asshole.

Diet

If you think we couldn't all improve how we eat.
If you think there's not also room to splurge every now and
then.
If you think all those fad diets aren't exactly that – a fad diet.
If you think those diets don't work for anybody.

Don't be an asshole.

Disabilities

If you think a disability means that someone can't do anything.

Don't be an asshole.

Disease

If you think someone on Facebook knows more than someone who's spent their entire lives studying them.
If you think that companies or governments would hide the cure to a disease to make money.
If you don't think there's plenty of other things to take from the people to make money.

Don't be an asshole.

Doctors

If you think someone on Facebook knows more than someone who's spent their entire lives studying them.
If you think I didn't copy and paste that last bullet from "Disease" on purpose.
If you think Doctors and Disease don't go hand in hand.
If you don't think you still need to trust your body when a doctor tells you nothing is wrong.
If you don't think a doctor has ever made a mistake.
If you think their batting percentage still isn't better than anyone else's.

Don't be an asshole.

Drinking

If you don't think an ice-cold beer or a glass of bourbon is
sometimes exactly what you need.
If you think IPAs should be so bitter your face falls off.
If you think it's ever worth it to drink and drive.

Don't be an asshole.

Driving

If you drive the speed limit in the left lane.
If you double park.
If you don't use your cruise control.

Don't be an asshole.

Drones

If you thinking fighting war without the loss of life isn't a
good thing.
If you think there aren't still going to be times when loss of life
is necessary.
If you don't think drones get us closer.

Don't be an asshole.

Drugs

If you think all drugs are bad for you.
If you think drug use should be punished to the highest
degree.
If you think there isn't a massive drug use problem.
If you think the government didn't have something to do with
starting it.

Don't be an asshole.

Economics

If you think socialism or communism is superior to capitalism.
If you think capitalism doesn't have its own problems.
If you think that the economy doesn't leave some behind.
If you think the government is the answer to fixing that.

Don't be an asshole.

Education

If you think education isn't the absolute key to a well running society.
If you think that the USA still leads the world.
If you think you can do better.

Don't be an asshole.

Electronics

If you think that electronics are just a government's way of controlling our mind.
If you think electronics haven't made our lives significantly better in every way.
If you think that humans have started to lose some of their humanity.

Don't be an asshole.

Environmentalism

If you think that this world, our only world, isn't worth protecting.
If you think the USA is the biggest or the only problem.
If you think the only way to solve it is to eliminate carbon emissions.
If you think it's possible to do that without going to war with the entire world.
If you think there will be anybody left to care if we do fight that war.

Don't be an asshole.

Feelings

If you think the world cares about your feelings.
If you don't think it should.

Don't be an asshole.

Food

If you cook your steak well done.
If you think food's only use is to provide nutrients and fuel.
If you think the food you like is the only good food in the world.

Don't be an asshole.

Fossil Fuels

If you think the world could run tomorrow without fossil
fuels.
If you think the world is going to need them forever.

Don't be an asshole.

Freedom

If you think Freedom of Speech means Freedom to Have
People Care.
If you think Freedom of Speech and Thought isn't a driver of
creativity and innovation.

Don't be an asshole.

Friendship

If you don't think some friends do and should grow apart.
If you think your significant other shouldn't be your best friend.
If you don't think a great friend is one of the most priceless things on earth.

Don't be an asshole.

Gender

If you think every one of the 7 billion people on earth must fall
into two categories.
If you think there needs to be a million genders.
If you think most of the ones you hear now aren't just made
up for attention.
If you think God cares.

Don't be an asshole.

Globalism

If you think the spread of money, language, and culture hasn't
improved us all.
If you think that it needs to stop.
If you think something that has proven to be so good is now
so bad.

Don't be an asshole.

GMOs

If you think we could feed the world without GMOs.
If you don't think it can still be scary.

Don't be an asshole.

God

If you think the God in your head is the God that should be in everybody's head.
If you think God wants to hear your plans.
If you think "faith" in God is the same as "proof" of God.

Don't be an asshole.

Government

If you think the government can do everything better than we can do ourselves.
If you think there isn't a role for government to play in the world.
If you blindly accept, or hate the current administration of government.

Don't be an asshole.

Guns

If your answer to violence is to add more arms to the equation.
If you think the way to fix violence is the complete removal of guns.
If you believe that guns play no role in violence.
If you believe that guns are an absolute right that shouldn't even be examined.

Don't be an asshole.

Hair

If you give a single crap what somebody else's hair looks like. If you don't think hair plays a role in presenting yourself.

Don't be an asshole.

Harassment

If you think anyone deserves to be harassed for any reason.
If you think friendly ribbing is harassment.
If you think that there are definitely black and white cases of
harassment.
If you think that there aren't also shades of grey.

Don't be an asshole.

Health

If you don't think your health is one of the most important
things in the world.
If you don't think part of the health equation is happiness.

Don't be an asshole.

History

If you don't think history repeats itself, or at least rhymes. If you think some history is worth erasing because it's uncomfortable.

Don't be an asshole.

Home

If you don't replace the toilet paper roll when it's empty.
If you don't take out the trash when it's full.
If you think you never need to leave.
If you think you can't always go home.

Don't be an asshole.

Human Rights

If you don't think every human deserves the right to life,
liberty, and the pursuit of happiness.
If you think it's somebody else's job to provide those for you,
and not just to avoid infringing on them.

Don't be an asshole.

Hygiene

If you don't think the strides in hygiene over the millennia is a
driver in the increase in life span over the millennia.
If you think it's your right to sacrifice others by neglecting
your own hygiene.

Don't be an asshole.

Immigration

If you think most of this country isn't directly descendant of immigrants.
If you think immigrants don't provide essential labor to the world.
If you think that that nearly all are coming here for the promise of being in the greatest country on earth.

Don't be an asshole.

Income

If you think everyone should make the same amount of
money.
If you think there isn't income inequality.

Don't be an asshole.

Inequality

If you think that every man and woman on earth should be afforded the same rights.
If you think that we as Americans aren't falling short of that.
If you don't think inequality needs to be constantly hunted and destroyed.
If you think you've lived in someone else's shoes.

Don't be an asshole.

Information

If you think information isn't now more accessible than ever.
If you think information isn't now more manipulated than ever.
If you think information isn't constantly changing.
If you don't think you need to change your opinions to fit any new information.

Don't be an asshole.

Intellectual Property

If you think a company deserves your intellectual property because you work there.
If you don't think intellectual property needs to be shared with the world.
If you think that the creator doesn't deserve the credit.

Don't be an asshole.

Internet

If you think that your memory is better than the knowledge
on the internet.
If you think the internet isn't one of the greatest disruptors in
human history.
If you think we're even close to scratching the surface of the
value of the internet.

Don't be an asshole.

Jobs

If you think every job is created equal.
If you can't understand how a janitor can take pride in their job.
If you don't think doing what you love can still be a job.
If you can't understand why some people just do it for the money.

Don't be an asshole.

Justice

If you think that you are a fair and impartial judge of justice.
If you think that there is little or no injustice in this country
and world.
If you think that it's never been worse or we don't need to
keep getting better.

Don't be an asshole.

Kneeling for National Anthem

If you don't think anyone has the right to do it.
If you don't think people have the right to not like it.
If you think those two things aren't the entire point of the
argument.

Don't be an asshole.

LGBTQ

If you can't see how this group is just fighting for rights that have been denied to them.
If you don't think the movement sometimes gets hijacked.
If you really think you care that much.

Don't be an asshole.

Loans

If you don't think that loans and debt can ruin your life.
If you don't think that they serve any beneficial purpose.

Don't be an asshole.

Love

If you think it's your place to choose who or what someone else loves.

Don't be an asshole.

Manliness

If you don't understand that there can be something fulfilling
about doing "manly" things
If you think that not doing those "manly" things makes
someone less of a man.

Don't be an asshole.

Marriage

If you think marriage can only be between a woman and a
man.
If you think somebody else's marriage somehow affects you.
If you think marriage is anything other than a religious
construct that's now co-opted by the government.
If you don't think that happiness with another is literally all
that matters.

Don't be an asshole.

Media

If you think that any major news media outlet is 100% truthful and reliable.
If you don't think that most media now a days is purely for ratings/money.
If you can't find anything out there that you like.

Don't be an asshole.

Money

If you think money can buy happiness.
If you don't think can help.

Don't be an asshole.

Monuments

If you think monuments to the losing side are anything but
participation trophies.
If you don't think a monument can and should bring attention
to history.

Don't be an asshole.

Movies

If you think movie writers aren't running out of ideas.
If you think there aren't still more ideas out there.
If you don't wish every movie theater had recliners and drink service.

Don't be an asshole.

Music

If you care what music someone else listens to.
If you've never been moved by music.
If you think music can't bring people together, and tear them apart.

Don't be an asshole.

News

If you think the news isn't completely biased.
If you think there is absolutely no unbiased news left.

Don't be an asshole.

People

If you cut lines.
If you literally put your kids on a leash.

Don't be an asshole.

Police Brutality

If you think cops should be defunded and eliminated.
If you think the police play no role in society.
If you think police can't also make mistakes.
If you think the police should not be held accountable for their actions.

Don't be an asshole.

Politics

If you think that you fall 100% towards the right or left.
If you think both sides don't have ideas that have merit.
If you think voting for who you want is a wasted vote unless it's towards a major party.
If you think one man/woman/child in politics isn't there to gain power.

Don't be an asshole.

Porn

If you think porn is the devil's work.
If you think it can't also lead to unreasonable expectations of
sex.

Don't be an asshole.

Prayer

If you think God acts on every little request.
If you think somehow it hurts to ask anyway.

Don't be an asshole.

Presidents

If you think one president can ruin and entire system of government or country.
If you think one party's president is a God, and the other is the Devil.
If you think any of them aren't just there to gain power.

Don't be an asshole.

Protesting

If you don't think the right to protest is critical in eliminating injustice.
If you think rioting is the same as protesting.
If you can't understand that sometimes it's going to come to that anyway.

Don't be an asshole.

Racism

If you think that racism is dead.
If you think that we aren't in the best place we've ever been.
If you think we can't still improve.

Don't be an asshole.

Reading

If you don't see any value in reading.
If you think the classics are the only good books.

Don't be an asshole.

Religion

If you think your religion is the only legitimate religion.
If you think that religion can't possibly lead to bad things, as well as good things.
If you think people haven't used religion to mask evil.

Don't be an asshole.

Renewable Energy

If you think renewable energy isn't the future.
If you think that it can replace fossil fuels 100%, today.
If you don't think that it's inevitable.

Don't be an asshole.

Rescue Animals

If you think shopping for an animal is a crime.
If you don't think rescue animals deserve a good home.

Don't be an asshole.

Revolution

If you don't think that revolution can be one of the most effective ways to change your world.
If you think it's easy to do right.
If you think a foreign government can force a people to revolt successfully.
If you don't think it has to be started by the people.

Don't be an asshole.

Rights

If you think Freedom of Speech means that anybody is
required to listen.
If you think Freedom of Religion doesn't also mean Freedom
from Religion.
If you don't think the Bill of Rights is a masterpiece.

Don't be an asshole.

School Shootings

If you think it's acceptable that this has ever happened – even once.
If you think that any right is so sacred that it shouldn't be studied to eliminate children dying.
If you think that means they want to take all your guns away.

Don't be an asshole.

Science

If you choose blind faith over science.
If you don't think that science is the pursuit of continual learning, and not a final answer.
If you don't think that the smartest person on earth once thought it was flat.

Don't be an asshole.

School

If you don't think a large chunk of school is a scam.
If you don't think it's still absolutely necessary.
If you think book learning is all school is about.
If you don't think school and learning needs to be constantly improved upon.

Don't be an asshole.

Sex

If you think anything on earth feels better than great sex.
If you think every time you've had sex it was great for the
other person.
If you think most of the time it you're not just doing it for
yourself.
If you think the best times aren't when you're doing it for the
other person.

Don't be an asshole.

Shopping

If you either hate, or love, shopping.
If you don't love that we can buy everything online now.

Don't be an asshole.

Smoking

If you think smoking isn't terrible for you.
If you think smoking a cigar or cigarette can't be relaxing.
If you don't miss a smoky bar every now and then.

Don't be an asshole.

Social Media

If you don't think social media caught traditional news media
completely off guard.
If you can't find enjoyment on social media.
If you don't think your brain needs to escape it sometimes.

Don't be an asshole.

Space

If you don't get overwhelmed thinking about it.
If you don't think it's incredible.
If you don' think out future as a species lies somewhere out there.

Don't be an asshole.

Sports

If you don't think that sports can unite a people, country, or world.
If you don't think sports can be one of the most frustrating and heartbreaking things on earth.
If you don't crave some sort of sport or competition.

Don't be an asshole.

Taxes

If you love paying taxes.
If you don't think that your tax dollars couldn't be spent
better
If you wouldn't much rather have your own money than give
it to the government.
If you can't understand that some of it is necessary.

Don't be an asshole.

Teaching

If you think teaching is easy.
If you don't think you have to love teaching in order to be any good at it.
If you think that all teachers love it, and that a large chunk aren't just there because it's the only job they ever saw.
If you think teachers don't deserve more.

Don't be an asshole.

Terrorism

If you think you can physically fight an idea.
If you don't think you can physically punish those
responsible.
If you can't see that the best way to fight terrorism is to make
them realize that it's better our way.

Don't be an asshole.

Travel

If you don't think there's anything to learn from the rest of the world.
If you don't sometimes urge to see other places.
If you don't wish that it was cheaper and easier.
If you don't take advantage of credit card points.

Don't be an asshole.

Vaccines

If you think vaccines cause autism.

Don't be an asshole.

Video Games

If you think violent video games lead directly to violence.
If you don't see how video games are just another form of expression.
If you don't have some nostalgia towards the classics.

Don't be an asshole.

Wall Street

If you think all Wall Street stands for is excess.
If you don't think in its current form that it's pretty damn excessive.
If you aren't confused by how people make money without making anything or providing any service.

Don't be an asshole.

War

If you think war is the best answer for nearly any problem.
If you don't think that a viable way to prevent war is to project overwhelming power.
If you think compromise isn't preferable to war in nearly every case.

Don't be an asshole.

Wealth

If you think anybody else is in control of your own wealth.
If you think inequality in the world isn't growing.
If you think there isn't a happy medium.

Don't be an asshole.

Conclusion

If you think the title **literally** meant "comprehensive".
If you're more pissed off than anything.
If you don't get the point by now.
Don't be an asshole

Buy, rate, and review – and thanks for reading! This is my first attempt at publishing a book and probably could be considered a trial run, but be honest in your reviews and maybe it'll help somebody figure out that most of the time when you get mad during an argument, somebody is just being an asshole.

Don't be an asshole.